Katie Not-Afr

Talks About Her Truth Queens and Story Bugs

Gina Marie Perkins

&

Delilah Joy Perkins

DEDICATION

Together, we dedicate this book to all the children out there who feel alone in their anxiety – and to the parents, caretakers, and educators, who desperately love them, and seek to know how to better support them.

ACKNOWLEDGMENTS

We'd like to acknowledge the main man in our lives, Zach. He has learned much more about anxiety than he likely ever wanted to, and has been a huge source of support and strength. We'd also like to thank the childhood psychologists who have made it their mission to understand children, and to equip them with tools that make them feel empowered and capable. To the educators who make their classrooms a safe and comfortable place for children with special emotional needs, we appreciate you. Finally, little sister, Zoey, thank you for always bringing your humor to the moment it's most needed. Being able to laugh at ourselves is a true gift.

And, believe it or not, we are so thankful to God for giving us the "Anxiety Superpower," because it's allowed us to see the world with more empathy and compassion.

Hi! My name is Katie Not—Afraidy, and I'm a pretty awesome girl!

I'm really great at exploring all kinds of art. I love to draw, and to paint – and I'm really careful when I'm using scissors. I even know how to use oil pastels! Of course I love stickers, glitter, and glue, too!

I'm also pretty daring when I ride my bike. I've raced on a real BMX track, where I even won a medal! I have to pedal really fast to get over the hills and jumps, which I guess means that I have really strong legs. You know what else I've done? I've driven an electric motorcycle that was just my size! I'm not even kidding...it's so much fun! Of course I always wear my helmet.

Speaking of my strong legs, I also love riding horses. Actually, I can't think of anything I'd rather do! The funnest part is when a horse trots (that's a fancy word for "jogs"), and my whole body bounces up and down on his saddle. Which is why you need strong legs, to hug the horse with, and to keep you from falling off!

I don't just love horses, though. I love all animals! I want to be a veterinarian, or a horse trainer, when I grow up. Right now, I have two cats, and two dogs. Sometimes I practice giving them check-ups, which they don't totally like. So, other times, I just give my stuffed animals check-ups instead.

Everyone says I'm a great chef, too. I always help my mom in the kitchen. My specialty is guacamole. My family says it's better than any served in a restaurant! I think it's because I mix in lime, salt, and mild salsa.

I can also crack eggs, flip pancakes, and make smoothies (I actually like adding spinach to my smoothies! Can you believe that?). I do love vegetables.

Oh, and I love school, too! I know how to read really well, and how to write short stories. I know many math equations, how to recite The Pledge of Allegiance, some Spanish words, and even a little bit of sign language. I learn new things everyday - even about exercise and nutrition. I've even learned how to play football during my recess!

I almost forgot to mention that I'm a big sister, too! My little sister is just two-and-a-half years younger than me, but I teach her so much. I'll admit it, sometimes it's hard to share my toys and games with her - but it's really awesome to have a friend who's always around to play with.

I'm just a normal kid who's creative, and compassionate, generous and smart. I'm kind, and polite, and a loyal friend. My parents say I'm respectful, and my teachers say I'm helpful.

What are some of your favorite things about yourself? I'm sure your list is long, too!

My mom and dad tell me that I'm also incredibly brave. I don't always believe them when they say that though, because, well, I have many worries.

And, my worries make me feel **afraid**.

Worries are like monsters that live inside my brain. They mostly come out at night, when everything is still and quiet. It makes it really hard for me to fall asleep, because they are loud and distracting. This makes getting up in the morning pretty hard, which can make it difficult to concentrate at school.

My mom told me that worries are normal, and even good and healthy. But, that my kind of worry is called "**anxiety**."

My kind of worries, or anxiety, not only make it hard for me to sleep at night, but cause me to sometimes want to stay home instead of play with my friends. Sometimes, anxiety stops me from trying new things, even if they actually sound really fun.

Lucky for me, my mom understands the difference between helpful worries and anxiety, because she has anxiety, too. She told me that it's like there are **Truth Queens** and **Story Bugs** living inside my brain (well, no wonder it's always so busy and loud in there)!

Truth Queens are the ones who tell the truth. When my worries start to take over my brain, I try to concentrate on what the Truth Queens are telling me.

For instance, I know that ghosts and goblins don't actually live under my bed. The Truth Queens reassure me that there's no such thing as monsters in my closet.

Then there are the Story Bugs, and they're absolute meanies! The Story Bugs are the creepy crawlies who make me doubt the Truth Queens. These bullies are the ones who tell me lies. Sometimes their lies start off as quiet whispers, but the more attention I give them, the louder they get. These Story Bugs tell me that ghosts are real. They convince me that my worries are really, really big and scary.

Do you have any Story Bugs living in your brain? What kind of lies do they tell you?

GHOSTS ARE REAL!

When the Story Bugs get really bold, they can sneak up on my happy thoughts like a ninja! I mean, out of nowhere, my worries can feel just like a karate chop! Like, everything in my brain is going great, and then HIYA!, my worries just knock out my joy.

Sometimes, it actually hurts. I get tummy aches, and headaches, and even chest aches. It can feel hard to breathe when the Story Bugs take over.

Other times, my worries are less sneaky than a ninja. Sometimes they start off slowly, and then start going round and round (and round and round), like a game spinner. It's almost like there's a wheel with different pie piece shapes on it. Each pie piece has a different worry on it, and whichever piece the spinner lands on, well, that's the thing that I start worrying about.

Talk about exhausting.

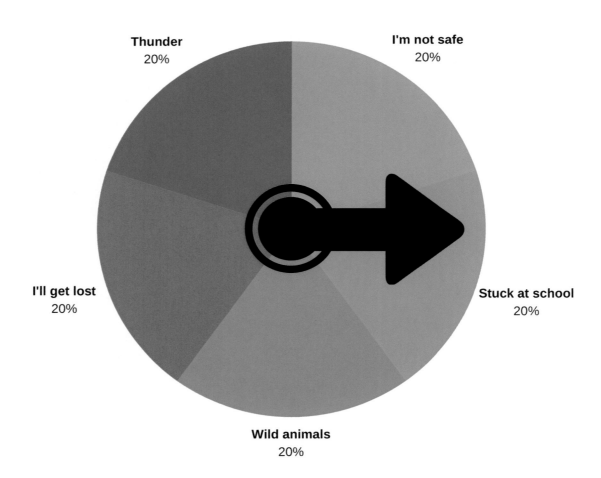

The Story Bugs can be so mean. It's like they sit in the corner of my brain, and wait for the worries to enter just so they can make them worse. My parent's don't typically allow me to use the "H-word," but I **HATE** the Story Bugs. A lot.

But, I have some good news.....I've learned that I can stand up to them. I can show them who's boss! I'm going to tell you more about that in just a minute, so stay with me, it's important stuff!

First, I want to tell you that I used to be kind of embarrassed of my anxiety. It didn't seem like any other kid had worries quite like mine. So, I didn't talk about it much. But, then it all got too big to keep to myself, and I started talking to my parents about it. That's when things started getting better. Not only did I find out that I'm not alone in having anxiety, but I started learning some cool tools to help me stand up to my Story Bugs!

Now, when I start to worry about things, I stop and take some deep breaths. It helps me to go somewhere quiet, so that I can sit, or lay, comfortably and not feel too distracted. I like to close my eyes because it helps me relax. And then I start counting, and breathing. I take a deep breath in through my nose while I slowly count to 3, and then I hold it for 2 seconds before I exhale for a count of 5. This slow breathing helps my body to know that I'm safe.

If you're reading this book with a grown-up, ask them to help you practice a few times. It feels so good, and helps my body calm down. Sometimes anxiety makes me feel jittery, or dizzy, or nervous inside. Breathing always helps take those weird feelings away.

Sometimes, especially at night, when the Story Bugs are busy in my brain, I like to listen to meditations for kids. Or, my favorite songs. If I practice focusing on the words in my music, my brain has less energy to also focus on the Story Bug lies.

Every once in a while, when music doesn't help, I'll just talk out loud to myself. I know it sounds kind of silly, but I'll tell myself that "I'm going to be OK." Once I say that out loud enough times, those lovely Truth Queens start saying it, too! Their truths get much louder than the Story Bug's lies.

See ya later, Story Bugs!

If I have a particular worry that I think about all the time (there was this one time, where every morning before school, I'd worry that I might throw up at school), I write it down on a piece of paper (you can ask a grown-up to help you if you're still learning how to write). Then, I fold that piece of paper up as small as I can get it, and I put it in my Worry Box.

Now, you might be wondering what a Worry Box is, so let me tell you. It's a special place (I use a wooden box that I painted. It looks like a treasure chest) where I tuck away all the worries that I write down. Once they're in the box, I feel like they're trapped in there, which helps me get them out of my brain.

And you know what I just recently did? I read through all those pieces of paper, and realized I didn't have those worries anymore, so I threw them in the garbage!

That felt so good.

Now, whenever I have anxiety, I just reach into my toolbox and pull out one of those tools to help me get through the hard moments. Some days, just breathing deeply works. Other days, I have to listen to good music, or even lock my worries into a box. And other times, I actually draw a picture of my worry, and call it names. It's the one time my mom lets me use bad words - like "dummy," and "stupid," and even "J-E-R-K." It makes me feel better to tell my anxiety how I feel when it makes me angry.

You can ask your grown-up which words are appropriate to use when standing up to your anxiety.

No matter how you get through your anxiety, the main thing to remember is that **it can't win**. Even when it feels like the Story Bugs are really strong, you have to remember that **you** and your Truth Queens will always be stronger. It takes a lot of practice, and you might feel frustrated, or afraid, or sad, at times – but, hang in there, it will get better. You can do this.

You know how I know you can do it? Because I did it. I learned how to love myself just as I am. So what if the girl who loves art, and sports, and animals, and school also has anxiety? It doesn't change just how awesome I am.

My parents were right, I am brave. I'm perfect just the way I am. I am Katie Not-Afraidy, and anxiety won't stop me from being exactly who I was created to be.

ABOUT THE AUTHORS

Gina Marie Perkins

Gina is a wife, mother of two daughters, and animal lover. She has had a love for writing since she was a child, and is thrilled to have partnered with her 8 year old daughter to finally publish a book that she's so proud of. Gina has also battled Generalized Anxiety Disorder for decades, and has built up quite a toolbox of her own. Though, nothing could've prepared her for the journey of helping a child through the throes of mental illness.

Finding hope through faith, community, awareness, and an unabashed voice of advocacy - Gina and DJ have found their way through anxiety, and consider their experiences as a gift to others.

Delilah Joy Perkins

Delilah, who prefers to go by DJ, is the amazing child in this book. She is all the wonderful and awesome things that Katie Not-Afraidy is. She is real, and she is brave. She is the motivation, and the inspiration, for this book. DJ is a doer of good, a lover of all, and a friend to many. She's pretty remarkable, really.

Made in the USA
Lexington, KY
05 December 2017